FRED's MAGIC ISLAND
S.O.Lessey
ILLUSTRATED BY MARTA SIECZAK

ISBN 978-1-953223-18-0 (paperback)
ISBN 978-1-953223-83-8 (hardcover)
ISBN 978-1-953223-88-3 (digital)

Rushmore Press LLC
1 800 460 9188
www.rushmorepress.com

Printed in the United States of America

3 MAGIC MARKET
EHLMWOOD MANGROVE
6
5 EHLMWOOD FOREST
2 PINEAPPLE PLAINS

In the Caribbean,
life is whimsical and carefree.
Raven plays in the forest
by a large cotton tree.

As night draws near,
Raven feels fear.
She went home to her Gran
who has a story
to share.

Onward to dream world,
Raven and Gran flew
To meet all the Guardian Spirits.
They'd know what to do.

4

Her pet Iguana, fred, stood
on the beach in the night.
He smiled, bowed. and gave
her a jar full of light.

6

Fred asked the stars for help,
to go from place to place.
A scarlet ibis,
red and bright,
landed in absolute grace.

"It is I, Anansi,
Guardian of the Lands.
Storyteller extraordinaire,
from the mountains
to the sands."

"I am Isabella,
the Warden of Art.
Sapphire, glass, and clay
come straight
from my heart."

13

"Billy's the name,
and I have special skills.
I could stand and walk on water!
It gives many the chills."

Tammy the Tamandua,
is an odd sight indeed
With her sharp claws
and long tongue
she protects any
forest in need.

This ride has been lovely,
we are almost done.
Times not up yet though,
we can still have some fun.

Raven dives with fred
and they dance in the sea.
The turtles, fishes, and octopuses
are happy to be free.

21

Phil is out for a party
in the middle of the night.
The crabs come out to play
while basking in the moonlight.

This journey is done.
It's time for bed.
Open the jar
and let the light dance
over your head.
25

The universe has feeling,
but sometimes needs healing.
Just look up above,
it made purely of love.

ABOUT THE AUTHOR

Shankarah Lessey

I am a writer born and raised in the Caribbean island of Trinidad and Tobago with a unique perspective on the world and its peculiar nexus with Caribbean culture, magic and history.

9 781953 223180